This edition published by Parragon Books Ltd in 2015 and distributed by

Parragon Inc.
440 Park Avenue South, 13th Floor
New York, NY 10016
www.parragon.com

ISBN 978-1-4723-9638-9

Printed in China

# A Perfect Picnic

Read the story, then turn the book over
to read another story!

Bath • New York • Cologne • Melbourne • Delhi
Hong Kong • Shenzhen • Singapore • Amsterdam

It was a beautiful spring day. The sun was shining, the birds were singing, and Mickey Mouse was planning a picnic!

The picnic basket was packed and Mickey and Pluto were ready to go. Suddenly, Mickey had a great idea!

"Picnics are so much better with company," he told Pluto.
"What do you think, boy?"

Pluto barked happily. He agreed with Mickey—everyone should come to the picnic!

Mickey picked up the phone and called Goofy.

"Hiya, Goofy," he said. "How would you like to have a picnic in the park? We can all bring our favorite foods, and then we can swap baskets!"

"Gosh, Mickey," said Goofy. "That sounds like fun! What should I bring?"

Goofy began to list his favorite sandwiches.

"Cream cheese and marshmallow? Pickle and honey?
Spaghetti and olive?" Suddenly, Goofy said, "I know
just what to make. See you at the park, Mickey!"

Mickey laughed as he put down the phone. This was
going to be an eventful picnic!

While Goofy made his lunch, Mickey went to invite his other friends to the picnic. First, he went to see Minnie.

"Oh, Mickey," Minnie said. "A picnic sounds like a perfect way to spend the day. And sharing all our favorite foods is a great idea. I can't wait!"

Mickey was on his way to Donald's house when he ran into Donald and Daisy taking a walk. He invited them to the picnic.

"A picnic sounds like a wonderful idea," said Daisy.

"I know just what to bring!" said Donald.

Donald raced home and began to pack his lunch.
First, he took out two pieces of bread to make a sandwich.
Then, he got out his favorite drink. Finally, he picked
some delicious, fresh grapes.

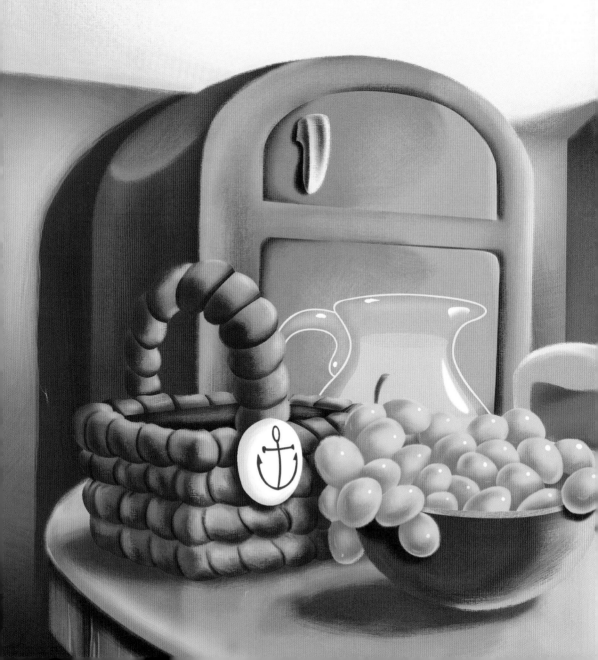

But, as Donald looked at the food, he felt hungry.
"These are my favorite foods," he said to himself.
"I don't want to share them. I want to eat them myself!"

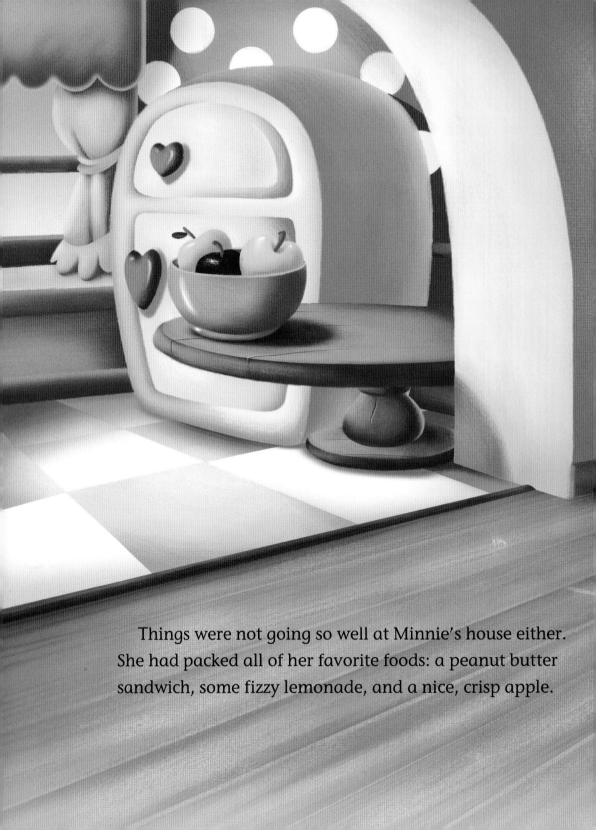

Things were not going so well at Minnie's house either. She had packed all of her favorite foods: a peanut butter sandwich, some fizzy lemonade, and a nice, crisp apple.

But as she got ready to leave, she began to wonder
if she would like the lunches her friends had packed.

"I don't want to share my lunch," she said out loud.
"I want to eat it myself!"

Daisy was excited about sharing her lunch.
"What a lovely day for a picnic!" she said to herself,
humming as she packed her favorite sandwich and drink.

Then, Daisy picked up a banana. Daisy thought about someone else eating her favorite fruit and began to frown. Maybe she didn't want to share her lunch after all. . . .

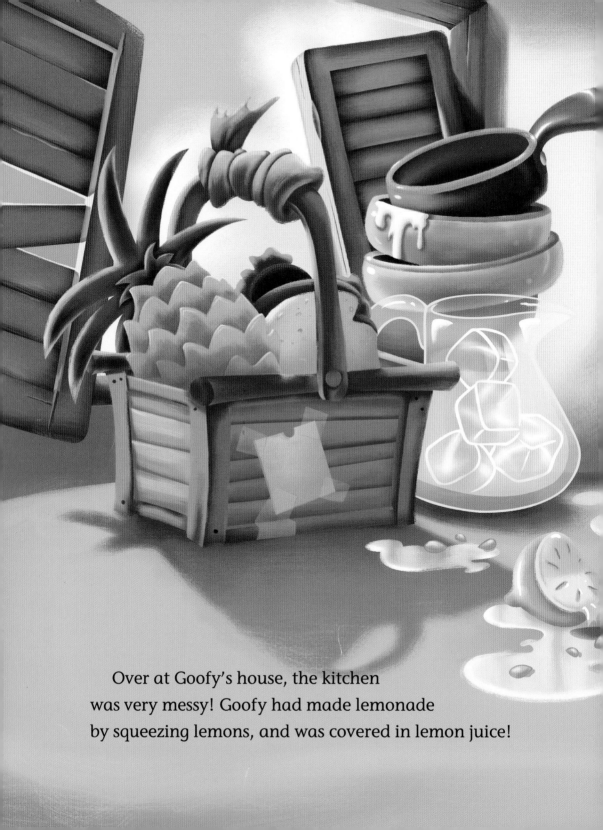

Over at Goofy's house, the kitchen
was very messy! Goofy had made lemonade
by squeezing lemons, and was covered in lemon juice!

Goofy tasted his lemonade. It was delicious!
"This is my best lemonade ever," Goofy said.
"I don't want to share. I want to drink it myself!"

Mickey had finished packing his basket and was
about to leave his house when Pluto began to bark.
He grabbed Mickey's shorts and tugged. "Woof!"
Mickey followed Pluto into the kitchen.

"Thanks for reminding me, boy," he said, taking out
a bone. "I wouldn't want to forget your favorite lunch.
Somehow, I don't think you'll have to share yours!"

As Mickey walked to the park with Pluto, he grew more and more excited about the picnic. He had no idea that his friends weren't feeling the same way.

"Won't this be fun, Pluto?" Mickey said. "I wonder what everyone packed for lunch."

When Mickey arrived at the park, he found Minnie, Daisy, Goofy, and Donald waiting for him.

"Hi, everyone!" he called happily.

His friends all had big baskets of food—but they didn't look very happy!

"What's wrong?" Mickey asked his worried friends.
"I don't want to share my lunch!" Donald admitted.
"What if I don't like the lunch I get?" asked Minnie.
"Bananas are my favorite!" cried Daisy.

Goofy nodded in agreement. Everyone wanted to eat their own favorite foods—and no one wanted to share!

"Oh . . . ," Mickey said, disappointed. "I guess we don't have to share."

Minnie looked at Mickey. He looked so sad!
She didn't want to be the reason he was upset.
   Minnie handed Mickey her picnic basket. "It's okay,
Mickey," she said. "I'll trade lunches with you."
   "Really? Thanks, Minnie!" Mickey said, delighted.

Mickey's friends saw how happy Minnie had made Mickey. They wanted to make him happy, too!

"Will someone trade lunches with me?" Donald asked, holding out his basket.

Daisy took Donald's lunch. Then she handed her basket to Goofy and he gave his basket to Donald. Everyone was sharing!

The friends worked together to set up
the picnic. Mickey spread out the picnic
blanket while Minnie passed out the plates.
Goofy handed out napkins while Daisy gave
everyone a cup. Finally, Donald set out forks.

Mickey opened his picnic basket first. When he saw what was inside, he started to laugh.

"What's so funny, Mickey?" Minnie asked. Then she looked in her picnic basket and started to laugh, too.

Everyone had packed peanut butter sandwiches and lemonade!

The only difference in the baskets was the fruit. Daisy had grapes, while Minnie had an orange, and Goofy had a banana. Mickey had an apple and Donald had a pineapple!

"Isn't there some way we can share our fruit? asked Minnie.

"I have a great idea!" said Mickey. "Leave it to me."

While his friends ate their sandwiches and drank their lemonade, Mickey cut up the fruit. He put it all in a bowl and mixed it together. He had made a big fruit salad for everyone to share!

"What a great idea, Mickey!" Minnie said as Mickey passed out the fruit salad.

"Now we can all try each other's favorite fruits!" Daisy added.

"This is the best picnic ever!" Donald exclaimed.

As Mickey's friends shared
their fruit and enjoyed dessert,
they realized Mickey was right.
Sharing was fun after all!

# The End

Now turn the book over
for another classic Disney tale!

Now turn the book over
for another classic Disney tale!

# The End

Mickey smiled and said, "Maybe we should wait
a little while. We could all use some peace and quiet."
And with that, he and Pluto settled down for a
well-deserved nap.

"Don't worry, boys," said Mickey as Minnie and Figaro drove away. "We'll tell her the whole story later, when she's not so upset."

"Please don't tell her too soon," begged Morty. "As long as Aunt Minnie thinks Pluto is a bad dog, we won't have to kitten-sit Figaro!"

Pluto and Ferdie nodded in agreement.

"I had hoped Figaro would teach Pluto some manners,"
Minnie said. "Instead, Pluto has been teaching him to misbehave!"

"But Pluto didn't do anything wrong," Ferdie said.

"It was Figaro!" cried Morty.

But Minnie wouldn't listen. She picked up Figaro and stormed off.

Suddenly, there was a loud clucking from the yard next door. Three frantic hens came flapping over the fence, with Figaro close behind!

"There's your sweet, little kitten!" cried Mickey. "He ran away last night and teased the ducks in the park. Then he broke the eggs in the dairy truck and—"

"And now he's chasing the chickens!" Minnie said.

Soon, Minnie arrived at Mickey's house.

"Where is Figaro?" she asked.

No one answered.

"Oh no, something has happened to him!" Minnie cried.

"Can't I trust you boys to look after one sweet, little kitten?"

Mickey and Pluto searched the whole town all night, but there was no sign of the missing kitten. By the time they returned home, the sun was starting to rise.

"Have you seen a small, black-and-white kitten?" Mickey asked the driver.

"Have I!" cried the driver. "He came running along and knocked over all my eggs!"

Mickey groaned as he paid for the broken eggs.

"Oh, Figaro!" he said. "Where could you be?"

Mickey and Pluto hurried to the pond, but Figaro wasn't there. Suddenly, Mickey spotted some small, muddy footprints leading away from the pond.

"Look!" cried Mickey. "They must belong to Figaro. Come on, Pluto. Let's follow them!"

Mickey and Pluto followed the trail of footprints to Main Street, where they met a dairy truck driver.

Mickey and Pluto made their way to the park down the street, where they bumped into a police officer.

"Have you seen a little black-and-white kitten?" Mickey asked the police officer hopefully.

"I certainly have!" he answered. "That little menace was teasing the ducks by the pond!"

First, they went to Minnie's house, hoping Figaro
had made his way home. But he wasn't there!

"Come on, boy," Mickey said to Pluto. "Maybe
Figaro went into town. He can't have gone too far!"

"You two stay here," Mickey told his nephews.
"Pluto and I will go and find Figaro."

Mickey and a very sleepy Pluto left the house
in search of the missing kitten.

Mickey and his nephews searched the entire house.
They looked upstairs and downstairs, under every chair,
on top of every table, behind every cushion, and even in
the yard. But they couldn't find the little kitten anywhere.

"Uncle Mickey!" called Morty from his bedroom.
"Did you remember to close the kitchen window?"

"Oh no!" cried Mickey, quickly jumping out of bed.

The kitchen window was open, and Figaro was nowhere
to be seen!

At bedtime, Figaro would not use the cushion Minnie had brought for him. Instead, he climbed into bed with Ferdie and tickled his ears with his tail! Finally, Figaro jumped off the bed and bounced into the kitchen.

At dinnertime, Pluto ate all his food like a
good dog. But no matter how hard Mickey, Morty,
and Ferdie tried, Figaro wouldn't touch the special
food Minnie had left for him.

Pluto growled at the naughty kitten, but
Mickey just sighed and cleaned up the mess.
"Take it easy, boy," Mickey told Pluto.
"Figaro is our guest."

Minnie was hardly out of sight when Figaro jumped out of Mickey's arms and ran into the kitchen. He pounced onto the table and knocked over a pitcher of cream!

"It's a good thing Figaro is staying with you," Minnie told Mickey as she got into her car. "Maybe he can teach Pluto how to behave!"

Mickey waved to Minnie as she drove off.

"Let's go, Figaro," Mickey said. "We're going to have lots of fun!"

Just then, Minnie and Figaro arrived. Minnie
was not impressed.

"Pluto!" she scolded. "Chasing chickens again!
You should be ashamed."

Pluto was ashamed, but only because the rooster
had chased him!

Before Morty and Ferdie could answer, they heard wild
flapping, clucking, and crowing coming from next door.
Suddenly, Pluto came racing across the lawn—with
a big, angry rooster chasing him!

"Guess what?" Mickey Mouse said to his nephews, Morty and Ferdie. "We're going to look after Minnie's kitten, Figaro, while she's away. Isn't that exciting?"

# The Kitten Sitters

Read the story, then turn the book over
to read another story!

## PaRRagon

Bath · New York · Cologne · Melbourne · Delhi
Hong Kong · Shenzhen · Singapore · Amsterdam

This edition published by Parragon Books Ltd in 2015 and distributed by

Parragon Inc.
440 Park Avenue South, 13th Floor
New York, NY 10016
www.parragon.com

ISBN 978-1-4723-9638-9

Printed in China